This Boo

D1321608

In the early hours of 7th September 1838
Grace Darling, the daughter of the
keeper of the Longstone Lighthouse,
saw a ship, wrecked and sinking on
the nearby rocks.

Braving the raging storm, she and her
father set out in the family rowing boat
and rescued nine people stranded on the
rocks. However, another rescue took
place that day – this one involved
Gracie and her kitten.

for James & Christopher

Rachel & Emma

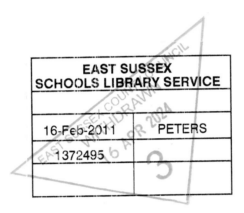

First published in Great Britain in 2010 by Andersen Press Ltd.,

20 Vauxhall Bridge Road, London SW1V 2SA.

Published in Australia by Random House Australia Pty.,

Level 3, 100 Pacific Highway, North Sydney, NSW 2060.

Text and Illustration copyright © Ruth Brown, 2010.

The rights of Ruth Brown to be identified as the author and illustrator

of this work have been asserted by her in accordance with the

Copyright, Designs and Patents Act, 1988.

Colour separated in Switzerland by Photolitho AG, Zürich.

Printed and bound in Singapore by Tien Wah Press.

Ruth Brown has used acrylic in this book.

10   9   8   7   6   5   4   3   2

British Library Cataloguing in Publication Data available.

ISBN 978 1 84270 971 9 (Hardback) ISBN 978 1 84939 026 2 (Paperback)

This book has been printed on acid-free paper

With thanks to the Grace Darling Museum, Bamburgh

GRACIE
THE LIGHTHOUSE CAT

Ruth Brown

ANDERSEN PRESS

Outside the storm was raging,
but inside the lighthouse
Gracie and her kitten were warm
and snug in the cosy parlour.

Gracie was sleepy – but her kitten was not.
When he heard the sound of voices and running
footsteps, he decided to go and investigate.

Down and down he went,
following the sounds . . .

. . . until he stopped at the front door. The gale force winds,
the driving rain and the huge, crashing waves were terrifying.
He turned to run back upstairs, when . . .

CRASH!

The wind caught the door
and slammed it shut, hurling
him out into the storm.

Gracie woke with a jump. She was alone. Where was her kitten? She called to him, but there was no answer.

She searched everywhere, all the way down
to the cellar, but still there was no reply.

Gracie climbed out of the cellar window.
She called and called to her kitten, but
her frantic cries were drowned by the
howling wind. It was hopeless.

Just as she was about
to give up her desperate search,
she saw something . . .

It was her kitten! Cold, terrified
and soaking wet, he was clinging like a
limpet to the slippery rocks.

Gently, Gracie picked him up and clawed
her way towards the safety of the lighthouse.

She climbed up the winding staircase,
back to the cosy parlour.

After a saucer of milk,
they snuggled down in their
basket by the fire.
Gracie was sleepy and,
this time, her kitten was too.

When news of the rescue was published in the *Newcastle Journal*, Grace became the media sensation of the day. She was awarded many honours, including the Silver Medal from the Royal National Institute for the Preservation of Life from Shipwreck (later to become the RNLI) and the Gold Medallion from the Royal Humane Society.

She never touched any of the money raised by public and royal subscription and continued to live a modest life with her parents at the Longstone Lighthouse, where she died in 1841.

Other books by Ruth Brown:

The Big Sneeze

Imagine

Night-time Tale

Ruggles

Snail Trail

Ten Seeds